MW01060092

QUICKREADS

BREAKING POINT

JANICE GREENE

QUICKREADS

SERIES 1

- Black Widow Beauty
- Danger on Ice
- Empty Eyes
- The Experiment
- The Kula'i Street Knights
- The Mystery Quilt
- No Way to Run
- The Ritual
- The 75-Cent Son
- The Very Bad Dream

SERIES 2

- The Accuser
- Ben Cody's Treasure
- Blackout
- The Eye of the Hurricane
- The House on the Hill
- Look to the Light
- Ring of Fear
- The Tiger Lily Code
- Tug-of-War
- The White Room

SERIES 3

- The Bad Luck Play
- **Breaking Point**
- Death Grip
- Fat Boy
- No Exit
- No Place Like Home
- The Plot
- Something Dreadful Down Below
- Sounds of Terror
- The Woman Who Loved a Ghost

SERIES 4

- The Barge Ghost
- Beasts
- Blood and Basketball
- Bus 99
- The Dark Lady
- Dimes to Dollars
- Read My Lips
- Ruby's Terrible Secret
- Student Bodies
- Tough Girl

ISBN-13: 978-1-61651-199-9
ISBN-10: 1-61651-199-0
eBook: 978-1-60291-921-1

Printed in Guangzhou, China
0310/03-20-10

15 14 13 12 11   1 2 3 4 5

■ ■ ■

Alana and Tiffany were heading toward the cafeteria when they heard the boys fall in close behind them.

"Notch, notch, notch," one of them said. His voice was soft and insulting.

Alana whirled around. *"What?"* she demanded. The taller boy smirked as he looked her up and down. The shorter one stared hard at Tiffany. His look was threatening.

"Hey—" Alana shouted, but Tiffany tugged at her arm to keep her quiet.

The boys followed them down the hall. Now they made wet smacking noises. The taller boy said, "Hey, Torres, looking good!

If you're lucky, baby, you'll be my next notch."

Alana stopped and faced them.

"Ooooh, Torres looks real mad now," the taller one taunted. "Protect me, guys! I'm scared to death!"

Alana clenched her fist. Her hand was strong from hours of basketball.

The girls quickly ducked into the bathroom. Derisive hoots of laughter followed them.

"What's *with* them?" Alana said. "What's this notch thing?"

"It's like a club," Tiffany said. "They put a notch on their belts for every girl they've gone out with. You just have to ignore them."

Alana was furious.

"Look, you're new here, so I'm telling you, Alana—don't mess with them. Especially that shorter guy, Chuy."

Alana remembered the way Chuy had looked at Tiffany. She started to speak, but then Marisol stuck her head in the door. "Come on, you guys," she said. "It's time for lunch."

Their friends were waiting in the

cafeteria. Seeing their smiling faces, Alana felt a warm rush of gratitude toward Tiffany. On her first day at Oceanside High, Tiffany had invited Alana to sit at her table at lunch. Now Tiffany's friends were hers, too.

Alana had just pried the lid off her yogurt when Chuy appeared at the head of the table. "Hey, Tiff," Chuy taunted. "I got something you're really going to like." He moved his hips. Alana got a good look at his thick black belt, which was cut with deep notches halfway around.

She glanced at the other girls. Tina and Marisol were talking, ignoring him. Tiffany stared at her sandwich.

With a flick of her spoon, Alana sent a gob of blueberry yogurt flying. It landed at the top of Chuy's zipper.

The girls broke out in nervous giggles. Chuy, his face contorted with anger, made a lunge for Alana.

But just then Ms. Martin, one of the PE teachers, strode up to her. "I saw you throwing food, Alana Torres!"

"He was hassling us!" Alana cried.

"Mr. Perez, you sit down! And you, Alana—anymore food throwing and you're on detention," said Ms. Martin.

As the teacher walked off, Marisol said, "Chuy's like the head of the Notch Boys, Alana. Don't make him mad."

"Oh, yeah? What can he do to me that's so terrible?" Alana grumbled.

"He'll spread stories about you. Real nasty stuff, believe me," said Tina.

"Last year this one girl, Briana, tried to get Chuy and another guy expelled," Marisol said. "They made it so bad for her that she had to leave. She goes to a different school now."

Alana looked at Tiffany, but Tiffany seemed very busy opening a package of cookies. Alana noticed that her friend's hands were trembling.

When the bell rang, Alana had barely finished her lunch. Alana and Tiffany left the cafeteria together.

“Want to come over after basketball today?” Alana asked.

Then, too late, Alana sensed someone moving up behind her. She looked back just as a boy grabbed the back of her skirt and flipped it up above her waist. Chuy did the same thing to Tiffany.

“Whoooo!” A chorus of hoots and cheers came from the kids who were walking along behind them.

Alana caught sight of the boys’ grins before they darted off through the crowd.

Alana blinked back tears of anger and embarrassment. “I’m going to the principal’s office!” she said to Tiffany. “Will you come with me?”

“Are you crazy?” Tiffany said. “Didn’t you hear what those girls were trying to tell you back there?”

“I’m begging you, Tiff. Will you come with me?” Alana said insistently.

Tiffany slowly shook her head. “Alana, if you want to fit in around here, there are certain things you just gotta understand,” she said.

■ ■ ■

"What's the matter with you? Why are you so scared of them? Why are you scared of Chuy?" Alana demanded.

Tiffany's face turned blank and cold. "I can't come over today," she muttered. Then she hurried away.

Alana walked into the principal's office. Mrs. Lachine was busy talking to the secretary.

Their conversation about a plumbing problem went on for several minutes. Finally, Mrs. Lachine noticed Alana and led her into her office.

The principal's face looked tired. "Is there a problem, Alana?" she asked.

Alana was telling her about the Notch Boys when the phone rang. After finishing a long conversation, the principal turned back to Alana. "Now, where were we?"

Alana's mouth tightened with frustration. She went on.

When she finished, Mrs. Lachine said,

"Don't worry about this notch thing. I'll talk to the boys."

"Right! My worries are over," Alana muttered to herself. She left the office feeling worse than ever.

■ ■ ■

Alana escaped to the gym. She hoped basketball practice would wipe out the disappointments of the day. Marisol met her at the door.

"Tiff quit the team!" she cried.

"Why?" Alana gasped.

"I don't know," said Marisol. "She just said she was tired of it."

"Tell me something, okay? Why's she so afraid of Chuy?" said Alana.

"Afraid? Sure, she watches her step around Chuy—like all the girls do—but I don't think she's *afraid,"* Marisol said. "A while back he was asking her out a lot. When she wouldn't go, he bothered her for a while, but I think he stopped."

"I'm going over there tonight—to see

what's going on," said Alana.

"That's good," Marisol said. "For some reason Tiff's been kinda down lately—but she won't say why."

When Alana rang the doorbell, Tiffany's brother Rich answered the door. He had a square, strong face and lively black eyes. He and Alana smiled at each other. Then she noticed the notches on his belt. "Is Tiff here?" she said coldly.

Rich smiled and made a deep bow, sweeping his arms out in the direction of Tiffany's room.

Alana marched past him and knocked on Tiffany's door. "Tiff, it's me, Alana," she said.

"Just a second," Tiffany called out.

Alana saw light appear at the bottom of the door. She realized the room must have been dark before.

"I just dropped in," Alana said. "I hope that's okay."

"Sure," said Tiffany. "Let's go in the living room."

As the door closed, Alana caught a

glimpse of Tiffany's room. What a mess! Every surface was covered with piles of clothes and dirty dishes.

They went to the living room, and Tiffany flopped on the couch.

"Hey, what's going on?" Alana asked.

"Nothing," said Tiffany.

"Come on, Tiff! Why did you quit the team?" Alana said.

"I just got sick of it," Tiffany said. "Too much work, day after day."

Alana wasn't satisfied with that answer, but she changed the subject. "Want to study for the math test?"

Tiffany shook her head. "It's a waste of time. I'm gonna flunk it anyway."

"Okay," Alana said patiently. "Want to go get something to eat?"

"I'm not hungry," said Tiffany.

"Tiff, come on! Are you mad at me or something? Do you want me to leave?" Alana asked.

Tiffany gave her a thin smile. "No, Alana—I'm glad you came," she said.

After watching TV for a while, Alana said goodbye. On the way out, she ran into Rich again. She scowled at him.

"Why are you so down on me?" Rich asked. "You don't even know me."

"You and all those Notch Boys act like animals," Alana snapped.

"Oh, lighten up! We're only kidding around. Why are you girls so uptight? You slap us down when we even look at you!" Rich said defensively.

"There's a big difference between harmless teasing and treating a girl like a piece of meat!" Alana said.

"Hey, not so loud," Rich whispered. But it was too late.

A door opened and a tired-looking woman in a bathrobe poked her head out into the hallway.

"Keep it down, will you?" the woman said in a groggy voice.

"Sorry, Mom," Rich said. Then he turned back to Alana. "Mom is trying to get some sleep. She works the graveyard shift," he explained.

"I better go," said Alana.

"Hey, what's your name?" Rich asked as Alana stepped out the door.

"Alana-Prime-Cut-Torres," she said sarcastically. If his mother hadn't been there, she would have slammed the door.

■ ■ ■

When Alana got home, Grandma was in the kitchen, chopping meat and vegetables for soup. Alana leaned on the counter, watching her. Finally, she said, "*Abuela,* some of the boys at school are awful. One of them pulled up my skirt today—right in front of everybody!"

Grandma smiled. "That means he likes you, *chica.* It's just what boys do."

Just what boys do. Alana's mom would have taken her seriously. But she was on a business trip and wouldn't be back for almost two weeks.

Tiffany wasn't at school the next day. When Alana stopped by the house after school, Rich answered the door again.

"If Tiff okay?" she asked.

"Yeah, she's okay, but she's got the flu or something. She says she doesn't want to see anybody," Rich said.

Alana was worried. "Is she sick—or just real depressed?" she asked.

"Depressed? I *said* she's got the flu," Rich repeated. But Alana saw doubt in his eyes.

"Has she ever talked about dying?" Alana asked in a soft voice.

"You mean like *suicide?* No! What a sick thing to say!"

"Couldn't happen to anyone *you* know, right? See you later," she said.

Alana saw Tiffany at school the next day. She ran up to her, smiling. Then she took a close look at her friend. Tiffany had dark smudges under her eyes. Her beautiful hair was messy, and she wore no makeup.

Something was *wrong*. "Hey, Tiff, are you okay?" Alana asked.

"People need to stop asking me that!" Tiffany said angrily. "Just leave me alone!"

She walked away. At lunchtime, no one could find her.

That night, Alana had been asleep for hours when the phone rang. It was Rich. "Tiff's gone!" he yelled into the phone. "Do you have a car?"

"Gone?" Alana mumbled. She was still half-asleep.

But Rich's voice was urgent. "Can you help me out? I gotta find Tiff!"

Alana's head cleared immediately. "I'll be there in ten minutes," she said. Grabbing the car keys and her mother's cell phone, she rushed out of the house. It was almost 1:00 A.M.

■ ■ ■

Rich was standing in the driveway when Alana drove up. "Thanks for coming," he said hurriedly, as he pulled her into the house.

Tiffany's mother was on the phone. As she listened she paced the kitchen, her voice high and shrill. "I *told* you," she insisted. "Long dark hair. Five feet one inch tall. I don't *know* what she's wearing!"

Tiffany's little sister Rina stood by the sink in her pajamas, looking bewildered. The kitchen clock said 1:08.

Rich turned to Alana. "Tiff left a note that said 'Don't be angry with me.' " He looked at Alana helplessly. Now he looked like a scared kid instead of a swaggering Notch Boy. His love and fear for his sister were plain on his face.

"How can I help? Where do you want to go?" she asked.

"I don't know," he said. "My uncle's looking downtown. Some friends are driving around the neighborhood—"

"Hmm. What's her favorite place?" Alana asked.

"The beach!" he said. "She always loved the water. . . . Oh, no!" His voice rose in alarm.

"Bring a flashlight!" Alana said.

Three minutes later, they were racing through the dark streets. Rich couldn't stop talking. "About an hour ago, Mom got up to go to work and the car was gone. We looked in Tiff's room and found the note. Then we found some pictures and letters—nasty stuff, really sick—that somebody's been sending her. Probably Chuy!" He swore. "I didn't even know!" he cried as he banged his fist on the dashboard.

"Well, of course Chuy wouldn't have told *you*," Alana said.

"It was right under my nose, and I didn't even see what she was going through!" Rich cried out bitterly. "You were the only one who guessed what might be happening," he added.

"Hey, don't chew yourself up about it," said Alana. "It's always easier for an outside person to notice things."

They reached the turnoff for the coast. "Which beach, do you think?" Alana asked as she looked around.

"Schrader's Point," Rich said.

They pulled off at the Point. In the dim light, Alana could see the waves breaking against the tall rocks at both ends of the beach. There was a single car in the parking lot. "That's ours!" Rich yelled. He quickly rolled down the window and cried out, *"Tiff!"*

The car door opened immediately. Tiffany hopped out and ran toward the rocks. Her long dark hair was flying behind her like a silky flag.

Alana braked and the car skidded to a stop on the gravel. She and Rich ran after Tiffany.

They saw that she was turning down a narrow path along the cliff. Rich and Alana were just a few yards behind.

"Tiff! *Stop!"* Rich called out.

But Tiffany kept going. She ran like the wind to the edge of the rocky cliff. For an instant she stopped there and looked back at them. Her hair was whipping wildly about her face.

"Tiff!" Rich yelled desperately. The pain in his voice tore at Alana's heart.

Then Tiffany jumped.

■ ■ ■

Rich and Alana ran across the top of the cliff. "Down here!" Rich cried out as he scrambled down the other side. Alana followed, her hands stinging as they slid against the cold, rough stone.

Rich stopped on a rocky ledge at the edge of the water. "You stay here," he commanded.

"No!" Alana said, starting to pull off her shoes.

"Please!" he cried, as he roughly grabbed Alana's arms. "I'll need you to pull her out of the water while I push."

She nodded and then watched as he yanked off his shoes and lowered himself into the water. After ducking under a wave, he bobbed up on the other side. Alana saw him swim forward a few strokes. But then his head blended into the darkness of the water, and he was lost from her sight.

A cold wave splashed against the ledge and sprayed Alana's jeans. She shivered and drew back against the steep wall of the cliff.

She waited, scanning the water beyond, and wishing she had kept the flashlight. As the minutes stretched out, she wondered if they'd *both* drowned.

Then Alana remembered the cell phone in her jacket. She pulled it out with frozen fingers and punched in *911.*

When the dispatcher answered, Alana strained to hear his voice above the pounding waves.

"Calm down, ma'am. Tell me where you are," the dispatcher said patiently.

"I'm at Schrader's Point. On this sort of ledge," she said, realizing how stupid she must sound.

Suddenly, she could see two dark heads bobbing just below her. *"Hurry!"* she yelled into the phone, before stuffing it back in her pocket.

Alana crouched down on the narrow ledge. When a wave pushed Rich and Tiffany toward her, Alana reached for Tiffany's shoulders. She felt Tiffany's hair brush against her hand—but then her friend was out of reach again, pulled back by the powerful tide.

Soaked and shaking with cold, Alana leaned out over the water as far as she dared. She braced herself. When the next wave came smashing in, she grabbed Tiffany's arm and held on. Then the wave pulled back, nearly wrenching Tiffany away. But Alana tightened her grip on the ledge and pulled Tiffany closer. Tiffany's head drooped forward, her eyes closed. Alana felt a stab of fear.

Rich's head bobbed up close by. As another wave rocked him forward, he struggled to push Tiffany up toward the ledge. Alana could hear him gasping.

Alana's teeth began to chatter. Her muscles ached with the cold.

Glancing up, she saw a new wave, white-tipped and taller than the rest, come bearing down on them. She tightened her grip on Tiffany's arm as the wave roared over them. Then Alana felt herself being swept off the ledge and into the water. Tiffany was gone!

Alana looked around. Now she was sobbing helplessly with fear and disappointment and exhaustion.

"Tiff!" Rich called, but neither one of them could see her.

■ ■ ■

Suddenly, the water around them was lit with a bright beam from above. Then they heard shouts and the sounds of people's heavy boots scrambling down the cliff.

A minute later, strong arms were lifting Alana from the water. "Get Tiffany," she said weakly. Then she closed her eyes.

The next thing Alana knew she was in some kind of vehicle, driving away. Voices floated above her. "Whose medication is this?" someone asked.

"It's my mom's," Rich's voice came out weakly. "She works the night shift, and sometimes she can't get to sleep."

Another voice said, "Looks like half the bottle is gone."

"We'll have to pump her stomach," said the first voice.

Then Alana heard the sound of coughing and terrible retching.

"Tiffany?" Alana cried out.

Someone put a firm hand on her shoulder. "Your friend is going to make it," a calm voice said. Alana closed her eyes again, feeling light with relief.

■ ■ ■

At the hospital, plastic bottles filled with hot water were packed around Alana. Then someone gave her something warm to drink. *Abuela* arrived and held her hand. Next door, Tiffany's mom was crying bitterly.

Alana drifted off to sleep. When she woke, all she wanted was to go home. *Abuela* was signing some forms when Rich appeared at the side of her bed.

"How you doing?" he asked.

"I'm doing okay," she said, trying to smile. "How's Tiff?"

"They said she needs to rest," he said. Then his voice tightened in anger. "I'm going to beat Chuy Perez so bad—"

"That's gonna help? *Come on!* You

think that'll actually do something?" Alana demanded.

"Yeah! He'll never mess with her again!" Rich insisted hotly.

"That's so stupid!" Alana said. "If you beat him, he'll just want revenge. And if he *really* wants to get back at you, he'll do something to hurt Tiff."

"If he does that, he's gonna pay big time!" Rich growled.

"Why not just get rid of him, Rich? Why don't we try to get him expelled?" Alana said softly.

"Ha! The school won't do anything," Rich said.

"Maybe you're right. But I've got another idea. I'll call you," said Alana.

■ ■ ■

The doctor ordered Alana to stay home and rest for a day or two. She used the time to work out her plan. First, she found an ad in the phone book: *Letitia Hernandez, attorney*. Then she called the number.

Yes, explained the secretary, Ms. Hernandez would talk to her, and yes, she sometimes took cases for free. That sort of legal work was called *pro bono*.

The next day, Alana sat on one side of a dark mahogany desk, and Letitia Hernandez sat on the other.

"Okay, tell me the whole thing, from beginning to end," the lawyer said, taking out a notebook.

When Alana finished talking, Ms. Hernandez snapped her notebook shut. "Ever hear of Title IX?" she asked.

Alana shook her head.

"It prohibits sex discrimination in schools," the lawyer explained. "In your case, discrimination would be severe student-to-student sexual harassment."

"Do we have a case?" Alana asked.

"I think you do. Attempted suicide would certainly indicate there had been severe harassment. And you say you have the notes this boy sent her. But I need to hear the story from Tiffany."

■ ■ ■

Tiffany was reluctant. "I don't know if I can deal with a lawsuit," she said uneasily.

Alana studied her friend's face. Tiffany still looked tired, but she'd curled her hair and put on makeup. Alana was encouraged. "Believe me, Tiff," she said, "the lawyer will handle most of it. She really seems to know what she's doing."

"I don't know, Alana," Tiff said. "Right now, I'd just rather forget about the whole thing."

"That's not going to happen," Alana said firmly. "You heard what Rich wants to do? He wants to beat Chuy to a pulp! Just come talk to her, Tiff. Then you can make up your mind."

Finally, Tiffany agreed to see the lawyer the next day.

"You probably felt so ashamed, you thought something was wrong with you," Ms. Hernandez explained. "But that's not true. This wasn't your fault. These boys made you feel so terrible, so worthless, that you wanted to kill yourself. They shouldn't be allowed to get away with that."

Alana saw Tiffany's eyes spark with anger. She wanted to cheer.

When the girls were on their way home, Tiffany said, "Let's take her suggestion. Let's call the other girls and see if they'll join in."

They started with Marisol. "That's cool!" Marisol said. "I'm tired of tiptoeing around school, always having to watch my back."

"Those creeps have ruled Oceanside High long enough!" Tina agreed.

By the time Tiffany's mom came home, eight girls had promised to join the lawsuit.

"Mom!" Tiffany said excitedly. "You know Chuy—the boy who sent me all that gross stuff? We found out that it was *illegal* for the school to let him get away with that. They should have protected me. So we called a bunch of girls and we're going to sue! We saw this neat lawyer—"

Tiffany's voice faded away. Her mother's face had turned as dark as a thundercloud.

"You are *not* going to sue!" her mother shouted. "Do you hear me?"

"Mom, *please*—!" Tiffany cried out.

"Don't you interrupt me!" Tiffany's mother yelled. "You know what lawyers do? They find out everything about you—*everything*—and they make it public! They dig up dirt and spread it around. I can't believe you actually went to see a lawyer behind my back."

Tiffany protested, "It wasn't like that! First, Alana went—"

Tiffany's mother turned on Alana. "How dare you involve my daughter in a scheme like this!" she snapped.

Alana gasped, "Mrs. Correa, Tiffany almost committed suicide!"

"She did *not!*" The mother's voice rose to a scream. "I never want to hear such a thing again. And if you spread rumors like that about Tiffany, I'll make you sorry. You're nothing but a little troublemaker! Now get out of my house!"

Alana grabbed her jacket and went to the door. The last thing she saw was Tiffany sobbing pitifully.

■ ■ ■

The next morning, Alana knew she couldn't put off school any longer. She reached in her closet for a skirt, then changed her mind and put on pants.

"I might as well put a bag over my head," she thought bitterly. "Those boys only see me from the neck down."

Alana ate lunch out on the bleachers, alone. She couldn't face Tiffany or her friends. She was crumpling up her empty lunch bag when Rich walked up, smiling.

"I've been looking all over for you! The lawsuit's on!" he announced proudly.

Alana stared. "Your mom said okay? I can't believe it."

"Yeah! Tiff and I worked on her for hours. Finally we said, 'What about Rina? She could go through the same thing as Tiff if we don't stop this.' I think that's what eventually got to her."

"It's really gonna happen? You're serious?" Alana said.

"Yeah!" Rich laughed.

They smiled at each other. Alana stood up, aimed, and tossed her lunch bag neatly in the trash.

Rich said, "Hey, Alana—you want to go out sometime?"

"Uh, I don't know, Rich."

Rich started unbuckling his belt.

"Just what are you doing now, Rich Correa?" Alana asked.

He slid his belt out of the loops and tossed it in the trash. "Just about all those notches were lies, anyway," he said. "Do you like me better now?"

Alana smiled. "I don't know yet. Only time will tell. Let's see how you *act.*"

He bowed low and offered his hand. She took it, laughing, and they walked back into school, hand in hand.

The first person they ran into was Chuy. He sneered at the sight of them. Alana's hand tightened on Rich's.

Chuy looked at them mockingly. "You hanging out with *her,* Correa?"

Alana turned to Rich. “Did you hear something?” she asked.

Rich held his open hand behind his ear, pretending to listen. “Nah,” he said.

They walked past Chuy as if he wasn’t there.

■ ■ ■

About two months later, Chuy really *was* gone. As a result of the lawsuit, he was finally expelled from Oceanside High School.

After-Reading Wrap-Up

1. What does the title, *Breaking Point,* refer to?

2. What did Alana bring to the beach that probably saved three lives?

3. Alana tells Rich her name is "Alana-Prime-Cut-Torres." What does she mean by that?

4. Of Rich, Alana, and Tiffany, which character did you like best? Why?

5. After Tiffany's suicide attempt, Rich wants to beat up Chuy. Why does Alana try to discourage him?

6. What if Tiffany's mom had refused to let the girls go ahead with the lawsuit? How might the story have ended?